Kids Can Press gratefully acknowledges the financial support of the Government of
Ontario, through the Ontario Media Development Corporation.

Published in Canada and the U.S. by Kids Can Press Ltd.
25 Dockside Drive, Toronto, ON M5A 0B5

Kids Can Press is a Corus Entertainment Inc. company

www.kidscanpress.com

English edition edited by Yvette Ghione

Printed and bound in Malaysia, in 10/2018 by Tien Wah Press (Pte.) Ltd.

MIX
Paper from
responsible sources
FSC® C012700

CM 19 0 9 8 7 6 5 4 3 2 1

Library and Archives Canada Cataloguing in Publication

Dekko, Espen, 1968–
[P+E. English]

Paws+Edward / written by Espen Dekko ; illustrated by Mari Kanstad Johnsen.

Translation of: P+E.
ISBN 978-1-5253-0135-3 (hardcover)

I. Johnsen, Mari Kanstad, 1981–, illustrator II. Title. III. Title: Paws and
Edward. IV. Title: Paws plus Edward. V. Title: P+E. English.

PZ7.1.E44Paw 2019   j839.823'8   C2018-904090-4

PAWS + EDWARD

ESPEN DEKKO
MARI KANSTAD JOHNSEN

E

KIDS CAN PRESS

Paws is dreaming.
Dreaming about rabbits.
He used to chase them.
Now he only dreams about them.

Paws is glad that Edward is reading.
That means he doesn't have to go out.
They go out twice a day.
That's more than enough for Paws.

"You okay, Paws?
Should we go outside?"
Paws wags his tail. Not too hard,
just enough for Edward to notice.

Paws is dreaming again.
About chasing rabbits.
And cats. And cars. And planes.
But mostly rabbits.

"Wake up, Paws. Let's go for a walk." Edward is ready.
Paws doesn't need to go out. But he follows along anyway.
Edward could use some fresh air, thinks Paws.

It's chilly outside.
Paws knows where they're headed.
His pace is nice and easy.
Paws doesn't feel the urge to run anymore.
He has run enough.

Sometimes on their walks, Edward
meets someone he knows.
Paws likes that. It means he gets to rest.

"Come on now, Paws.
You can't stay here.
We have to keep going."
Paws completely forgot
they were on a walk.

The park is empty.
No smells. No noises. No rabbits.
Edward throws a stick.
The stick disappears into the trees.
Edward searches. Paws waits.

Where are all the rabbits? thinks Paws.
And the birds? And the other dogs?
Edward has found the stick.
"Are you tired, Paws?"
It feels good to lie in the grass.
Together with Edward.

Paws has walked and walked. His paws are heavy.
Paws doesn't have to walk anymore.
Paws doesn't have to do anything anymore.

Edward's bed is warm and cozy. Like rabbit fur.
Paws sleeps and sleeps. Sleeps and dreams.

Edward calls for Paws.

Paws pretends not to hear.

He isn't thirsty.

He isn't hungry.

He doesn't want to go out.

All Paws wants to do is lie in Edward's bed.

And dream.

Paws can feel Edward's heart beating.
Edward is being so strange. His eyes are wet.
Paws licks his hand. Edward needed that.
And then Paws falls asleep.
A sleep without dreams.

Paws's spot is empty.

His dish is in the cupboard. Empty.

The house is quiet.

Too quiet. Edward can't read.

He goes outside. For a walk. Without Paws.

Everything is there. The smells. The noises.

Even the rabbits.

But not Paws.

Edward is dreaming.
Dreaming about Paws.
Paws is happy. He barks and wags his tail.
Finds sticks. Chases rabbits.
Just like before.